Where the Hell is Heaven?

Also by Ian Coulls and published by Ginninderra Press
The Complete and Utter Truth About the World and Everything In It
Danse macabre (Pocket Poets)
Words (Picaro Poets)

Ian Coulls

Where the Hell is Heaven?

Acknowledgements

I would like to express my gratitude to Stephen Matthews of Ginninderra Press, Anthony Priwer, Kate Ryan, Sharon Kernot, Amy Yang, Pam Illert, Shirley Jansen, Ray Clift, Gareth Saunders, Christina Barrie, Lorna Lower, Jenny Liu, Kensington and Norwood Writers Group and North Eastern Writers Inc for their editing, advice, help, support and encouragement.

First published 2017 by
GINNINDERRA PRESS
PO Box 3461 Port Adelaide 5015
www.ginninderrapress.com.au

Contents

Hell in Paradise

Bucky Armitage was a young Englishman working in China. He was an English teacher in a Guilin university. It was an idyllic posting as Guilin is regarded by many Chinese people as heaven on Earth. As seen on postcards, it is the place with the dome-shaped hills and old men with pointy hats. On their bamboo rafts, these men go fishing with trained cormorants. Bucky and his wife Meihua agreed Guilin was paradise.

The Guilin foreign teachers would periodically organise Friday night social gatherings in the Sportsman's Bar of the Shangri-La Hotel. On one of these evenings, Bucky and Meihua walked in to relax with the various teachers, their wives and girlfriends. Amongst the group was Nigel, who had come from London as a representative for MG sports cars. He zeroed in on Bucky and Meihua and they all exchanged initial pleasantries.

'So do you often go back to England?' Nigel asked.

The question was addressed to Meihua, but she was neither listening nor interested. She had turned away and was talking to a Chinese friend.

Bucky replied, 'Every so often, but only for the holidays. We've just come back, actually. What do you do in London?'

'Car salesman. 'Ere, if you ever come back to live, let me know if you need a car. I can really look after you. I don't sell rubbish or nothin', you know, only quality stuff.'

'Yes, of course, thanks, but I think we're likely to be here for a while yet. Meihua rather likes England, but it's so expensive, and my English job was OK, but rather boring.'

'What did you do?'

'Computer programmer.'

'Ooh, you must be sophisticated. Still, this is a bit of all right here in China, isn't it?'

'Well, we like it. Meihua wouldn't mind living somewhere nice in the south of England, but that's a way down the road yet.'

Meihua was still talking to her Chinese friend and Nigel's conversation became a little more adventurous.

'The women are nice here in China, eh? 'Ere, look at that,' he drooled. 'Do you ever step out for a bit on the side?'

'I'm married,' Bucky reminded him, maybe aware that Meihua was still sitting next to him, although his answer probably would have been the same if she had been in Siberia.

'Yes, I know, but I mean, well, you know what I mean...' Nigel enthused. 'Cor, who's that?' he asked, pointing out another attractive Chinese woman.

'That's Xi Huanjing. She teaches French but, when she's had a few drinks, she tends to forget she's a teacher. Her students quite like her.'

Xi Huanjing was full of beer and covered with students.

'Obviously, but I'm not surprised. With an arse like that, she'd have the attention of every boy in the class when she writes on the board. Do you think she could do with some adult company?'

'Why don't you go and ask her?'

Bucky was relieved when Nigel picked up his beer and made his way toward the young woman. His relief was interrupted by Chris Bligh, a balding, middle-aged man who, for some reason, everyone called Tubby.

'Hello, Bucky. Have a good holiday?'

'Yes, fairly laid-back, and it was good to catch up with family. I hear you moved into Scott's apartment.'

Bucky immediately winced inwardly. A thoughtless slip. Chris Bligh's real estate grab had annoyed staff, as he was a recent arrival and the apartment was coveted by all the teachers. He had thrust himself forward and snaffled up a post as representative for the foreign teachers and then rapidly claimed the much-envied apartment when its previous inhabitant went back to the United States. Some teachers had been in Guilin for years and felt they had a much more justifiable claim.

'Hey, someone had to do it.'

'Are you coming to any of the Chinese classes?' Bucky asked. Foreign-language tutors were entitled to go free of charge to any of the fee-paying Chinese lessons.

'Why bother? They have to learn English. I don't have to learn Chinese.'

'Come on, Bucky. Let's go home.' It was Meihua, tugging at his sleeve.

Bucky was ready to leave.

As they made their way to the door, Bucky noted that Nigel had replaced Xi Huanjing's students and was providing the adult company he felt she needed. He had his arm around her and was earnestly explaining some issue that she was not going to remember in the morning. She was not aware of the unfortunate angle of Nigel's glass of beer. It didn't matter. If he spilt any beer on her, she probably wasn't going to notice. As Bucky and Meihua walked out, Tubby was still drinking at the bar.

*

Tubby had already cornered another victim who could benefit from his company and his thoughts. He didn't know anything about Gong Anju, who had been sitting alone further up the bar. On the other hand, Gong Anju knew a fair bit about Tubby. She knew a fair bit about everyone. She worked for the Public Security Bureau.

In conversation, Gong asked questions that seemed to spring not from general interest, but from the compilation of some sort of dossier. Not really questions, more an interrogation. People who knew about her job steered clear of her, and those who didn't know her moved on fairly quickly anyway. They didn't like her inquisitive nature and her pushiness.

Gong Anju had no interest in Tubby at all, but she had been watching Nigel, who was busy with Xi Huanjing. The public security issues arising from this woman's relationship with a foreigner could possibly merit closer investigation. There would be no need to mention that recent evening when Nigel had taken advantage of Gong in a hotel room and had left the scene within half an hour. Needless to say, his rapid departure had displeased her.

*

The early morning light had turned the bedroom to a dull grey and Bucky rolled over to escape the arrival of the new day. Meihua was beside him and only half asleep. She mumbled gently and curled into his arms.

He put his arm around her and she mumbled again, 'Bucky, when are we going to have a baby?'

'I don't know, dear. We've talked about it before. You wanted to get that jade bracelet, so we haven't got a lot of money at present. And there's still the monthly payment on the new apartment. They haven't even finished it yet and then we have to fit it out. Maybe in a couple of years we can start thinking about it.'

Although the university job included free use of a campus apartment, Bucky's parents had lent them the down payment on a plush apartment that Meihua said they needed, an off-campus apartment, which was neither finished nor furnished. Some of Bucky's friends had been indiscreet enough to point out that he was not Chinese, Meihua was, and Chinese law was Chinese law. In alcoholic moments, they had suggested to him that, should the marriage fall apart, he might have difficulty getting much of his money back.

'Do you think we need to wait that long?'

'Let's not talk about it now, love.'

'No, but –'

'Go to sleep.'

'I want you…'

'Have you taken your pill?'

'Of course.'

Any remaining thoughts of sleep disappeared.

There was, however, one thing that she hadn't told him. Given her lack of success in convincing Bucky about the breeding plan, she had stopped taking the pill some six months before. In the event of her pregnancy, she just would have said there had been an accident, and hey, anyway, they were always going to, so they would just have to accommodate an earlier arrival than planned. Unfortunately for Meihua, this course of action had not produced results. She knew that one of them was lacking but, given the deceptive nature of her strategy, she was not able to discuss it with Bucky.

*

Earlier that night, Nigel lay looking at Xi Huanjing by the light of a bedside lamp. It was midnight and she was asleep. A long evening of drinking had taken its toll. For Nigel it had been an excellent evening. Xi Huanjing was warm and fun-loving and her lovemaking had been drunk and vigorous, too vigorous in fact, bringing Nigel to a happy ending well before she herself had reached any level of satisfaction. In Nigel's world, this mattered very little. She was attractive and he had shagged her. She was just another trophy on his mantelpiece and he had no thoughts of a continuing relationship. He got up quietly, dressed and left. He didn't see Gong Anju sitting in an unmarked car across the road.

*

It was now Saturday and by mid-morning Bucky and Meihua were shopping at their local market. Influenced by a couple of extra glasses of red wine in the Sportsman's Bar the previous evening, Meihua had invited everyone to their place that night.

Bucky didn't enjoy the marketplace. You needed to haggle. He had to confess his limp haggling probably disappointed some vendors. Usually, if he didn't like the price, he just moved on and the vendor didn't get a second chance.

If Meihua came with him, it was more confrontation than a polite Englishman could endure. She would pick everything up, feel it, sniff it, inspect its private parts, and point out its blemishes and deficiencies. This would set the framework for some full-frontal haggling.

Bucky couldn't pretend he didn't know her, because everyone in the market knew they were married. He had wandered off, investigating some different fruit he hadn't yet tried, when he became aware that Nigel was standing beside him.

'So Tubby tells me you're having a bit of a gathering this evening?' It was a question as much as a statement. To put it more exactly, it was a request to be invited.

Bucky was too polite not to oblige. 'Yes, didn't anyone tell you? You'll come, of course?'

'Well, great, thanks. Yes, of course.'

'Why don't you invite Xi Huanjing?' He realised too late this might have been indiscreet.

'Yes, well, I think she's busy tonight. We'll see how it goes,' Nigel replied, not quite lying, but hedging his bets. He didn't know how his early departure from her bed had been received. He usually left quickly because he knew that waking up next to someone in the morning often involved conversations about tomorrow and the next day and the future. If Xi remembered the previous night's lovemaking, she probably wouldn't come anyway.

'It's not dinner, but there'll be plenty of food during the evening,' volunteered Bucky, anxious to help fill what might have been an embarrassing gap in the conversation.

'What's this?' Nigel asked, picking up a mysterious spiky fruit in front of him.

'Don't even think about it. It's a durian. They smell like old socks, and lots of hotels won't even let you bring them in.'

'So we won't be able to try any of these tonight?'

'You can bet on it.'

*

Nigel had brought his nylon guitar to the party. He had infinite confidence in his talent and was sure people would like it, especially his rendition of 'Purple Haze'. The older Westerners recognised and enjoyed it, even though it lacked the accompanying drums and bass. Most of the Chinese people hearing it, including many of the younger ones, thought it was a lot of meaningless noise. Eventually, Nigel took a break and went into the kitchen to get another beer.

'So how long have you been playing the guitar?' Meihua asked.

'Since I was about ten.'

'Does it take long to learn?'

'Not long to get the basics, longer to play as well as I do.'

'How much would you charge to give me a few lessons?'

'You, luv? We could work something out. You would never play as good as me, but you could still play pretty good.'

'How about a couple of lessons for free, just to see if I want to go on?'

'Oh yes, why not?'

Bucky walked in to get another beer. 'So what happened to the music? Have you gone on strike?'

'No one brought me a beer.'

'What's the world coming to? You'll have to speak to the union about this.'

'Darling, Nigel's going to give me some free guitar lessons.'

'Just for a start,' Nigel interrupted quickly. 'Just to see if it's worth going on.'

'Nigel, you have a way with words,' teased Bucky. 'You should be a diplomat. Does this mean we're going to have to buy you an electric guitar, Meihua? We can't put it through an amplifier. The neighbours won't be happy.'

'I'm sure Nigel will let me use his guitar till we find out if I'm any good.'

'Well, you'll need your own guitar to practise,' Nigel said. 'I'll need to take mine home with me.'

'Yes, but just for a lesson or two so we can see if I want to go on?'

'OK, I don't see any problem there. When would you like to try?'

'How about late next Saturday afternoon?' suggested Bucky. 'We can have a few beers and Nigel can stay to dinner.'

'Oh no, darling! It'll be too embarrassing if you're there. I just want to find out first if I can do it.'

'Oh well, I'll leave it to you two to organise yourselves.' Bucky went back into the lounge to rescue Gong Anju and her husband from one of Tubby's diatribes.

*

'No, here, like this.' Nigel adjusted the position and angle of the guitar on her thigh. 'And drop your wrist here, so your hand comes around the front, and your fingers come down vertically on the fingerboard.'

'Like this?'

'Yeah, almost. Here, pass me the guitar and I'll show you.' He modelled the required position and passed the guitar back to Meihua.

'Is this right?' she asked.

'Better. Just drop your wrist and bring your hand around to the front a bit more.'

'How's this?'

'Here, let me show you.' He came around to the back, leaned over her shoulder and gently took her wrist, but couldn't move it. 'Relax. You're too tense. Here, keep the neck of the guitar up or you'll have to lower this left shoulder.' In fact, he liked it when she dropped her left shoulder as it opened her shirt slightly, revealing breasts that were raised and accentuated by the body of the guitar. 'Here, relax. You're all tense.' He gently massaged her neck and shoulders. 'Relax, relax.'

'I can't help it. This seems like such an unnatural position.'

'Here, just put the guitar down for a second.' He took the guitar from her and placed it safely in the corner. 'This happens to everyone. We'll just relax those muscles and you'll find it much easier.'

An hour and a half later, Nigel left the apartment and Meihua felt slightly more relaxed, although her guitar lesson had not advanced beyond that point. She was relaxed because Nigel had left, not because of anything else that had happened. She got up and made the bed, wrapped up an unused condom that Nigel had left behind, and threw it in the bin. She had assured him he wouldn't need it, as she was on the pill. Nigel was happy, as he put it, to go diving without a wetsuit. He was sure Meihua didn't share herself around too much.

Nigel was a happy man, but Meihua had very mixed feelings. Infidelity was not something that sat comfortably with her, either culturally or personally. Nigel had not been the lover he believed himself to be. Despite his conviction that he left a trail of female pleasure behind him, he had been hasty and ungainly in both the mount and the dismount, leaving Meihua knowing that Bucky was a far more caring and enjoyable lover. The relationship would be brief, she hoped: just till her next period or lack of it.

Although she didn't normally drink it, she made herself a coffee. Even before the coffee, her heart was pounding. Bucky would be home soon. She would have to invent stories about progress she hadn't made on the guitar. She made excuses not to demonstrate this progress. Her afternoon enterprise had not been something she had taken lightly. She was riven with guilt. She loved Bucky and had never been unfaithful before. She had never given herself to anyone before Bucky. Would he be able to tell? Would he see it in her eyes?

Meihua told herself she was doing it for both of them. There would be a child and, although Bucky didn't want it yet, he would love it. Nigel was English too, so anything un-Chinese about the child's appearance would be attributed to Bucky. She just hoped she wouldn't have to do this thing with Nigel too many times. She tried to push away memories of his searching hands and hungry mouth. She got up and made another cup of coffee.

Nigel made five more visits before she knew she was pregnant and could tell him she thought guitar was too difficult. Although she would have liked to explain his dismissal more imperiously, she was not foolish. She didn't want any ill will that might complicate the issue. She told him that although he was a good man and a wonderful lover, she was committed to Bucky and she was unable to cope with the guilt of a continuing relationship with someone else. She would have loved to tell him he was an arrogant little turkey with the lovemaking finesse of a mud buffalo, but she knew that would not have been a wise move.

*

Meihua had made a special dinner and bought one of those bottles of supposedly French wine with the incorrect spelling on the label. The meal had been relished and the wine was being savoured when Bucky sat back in his chair.

'OK, so what's the special occasion?'

'Well… I went to the doctor's today…'

Bucky was instantly nervous. You don't have a special meal with fake French wine because you have diarrhoea.

'Oh, oh…'

'I'm pregnant, Bucky. We're going to have a baby.'

'Oh Jesus, we can't afford that!'

'Yes we can, dear. It's OK. I can get work too if we need to. Anyway, your parents will help. They're always great.'

'I don't want to be always asking Dad for money. We've already done it way too often.'

Tears welled up in Meihua's eyes. 'Bucky, this is our child and you just want to talk about money!'

'Honey, it's great about the baby, but you're the one who wanted the apartment and the jade. It's just that someone has to pay for it all.' He put his arms around her and held her close.

Now the battle was lost. Meihua always won from this position. She was so petite and snuggled up so close. It was all over.

She explained to him how she could go out and work, and her parents could come and live with them. Her parents could look after the child while Bucky and Meihua were at work. Bucky was not convinced. Maybe it was selfish, but life was better with just the two of them. He knew his parents would be willing to help and he liked Meihua's parents, but he didn't want to live in an extended family situation.

*

Meanwhile, Nigel could not be relied on to be honourable. What was the point of conquest if no one knew about it? Tubby was always open to sleaze and so Nigel's little tale of conquest had found its way into their conversation, just in passing, mind you. It wasn't as if he was boasting or anything. Tubby had laughed and bought Nigel a beer. This gave him the opportunity to recount a tale about one of his own conquests, real or imaginary, just in passing, mind you. It wasn't as if he was boasting.

Within weeks, Tubby, with too much blood in his alcohol stream, had, in passing, made some snide remark to Gong Anju in the Sportsman's Bar about Meihua's supposed guitar lessons.

Gong was not likely to tell Tubby, 'Hey, he shagged me too.' Convincing herself that it was nothing to do with personal jealousy, Gong felt this was an issue of public morality. She decided she should investigate further before acting, but by this time, Tubby had already smirkingly suggested to Bucky that Meihua was getting help from someone else.

'So what do you mean it's not mine?'

'It's not yours.'

'What do you *mean* it's not mine?'

'It's someone else's.'

Meihua was calm, but Bucky's voice had diminished to a husky whisper. 'Whose is it?'

'It doesn't matter.'

'Of course it matters. We're married!'

'So it's our child.'

'How can it be our child if it's not my child?' Bucky knew the answer, but didn't want to know.

Meihua stood immobile, silhouetted at the window. She had feared for some time that this conversation might come. She was prepared. She had rehearsed it in her mind so many times.

For Bucky, this was the first time. He was totally unrehearsed. He had never read the script. He had heard the story before, but had never imagined he would be cast as a co-star. Meihua said nothing.

'Well, who's the father?'

'You don't need to know. It won't change anything. I don't love him. I don't want to know him.'

'What? And you think that's OK? Well, it's not OK with me!' Bucky felt he was losing control, and didn't want to say or do anything silly. He desperately needed time to think. He turned and walked out, slamming the door behind him.

He went walking in the university grounds. It was a beautiful, brisk morning with a clear, blue sky and frost on the grass. He pulled his muffler higher and thrust his hands deep in his pockets. His heart was throbbing. Everything inside him was bleeding. Tears of bitterness stung his eyes and ran down his cheeks. When had this happened? How long had it gone on? Was it just one disgusting moment when she had let someone do the dirty deed, or had there been a relationship?

He couldn't imagine which would be worse. It all escaped him. And so what were his options now?

Bucky was bereft. He had thought their happiness was already complete. Just to be with Meihua, just to share his life with her was already enough. He felt he had given everything to their relationship. That she should bring another man into their life was unthinkable.

Was he being old-fashioned? Maybe, but he could not go on like this. Should he leave her? He couldn't imagine his life without her. He remembered his friends saying she could end up with everything: the apartment, the jade, the child, everything. He knew he could live without those things, but, without Meihua, it would be a bleak, colourless life.

Gradually the reality dawned on him. What was done was done and he knew, although it was common in China, he couldn't ask her to terminate the pregnancy. Much as he thought it repulsive, he realised that he could, he would have to, accept what had happened. He would tell her he still loved her. He would accept the child as theirs, but he would make it clear that she could have no further contact with this man.

*

When Nigel had indulged in his brief carnal interlude with Gong Anju, his interest had not extended as far as asking what kind of work she did. He was, therefore, more than a little surprised when she arrived at his door in uniform. The male officer accompanying her explained that there were irregularities concerning Nigel's visa and residential permit. Gong explained what the consequences might be, but that, although these were matters of concern, they were only part of a broader spectrum of moral issues being investigated. His case could be considered in a far more favourable light if he were able to help with these other enquiries.

Nigel was only too willing. He admitted his evening with

Xi Huanjing and his relationship with Meihua. He didn't know that sexual relations with a married person is a crime in China. As it had been Tubby who had told Gong about his relationship with Meihua, Nigel was massaged for further information about Tubby. He remembered that Tubby had boasted of one of his own illicit escapades. When further questioned whether this adventure had been with Meihua, Nigel claimed he was uncertain, as Tubby and he had both been drinking. With gentle persuasion, he was willing to make a signed statement about the events. It mattered little whether the tale was true or not. He merely stated that Tubby had told him.

Not surprisingly, shortly after this, Tubby had a visit from Gong and her partner. They explained that these were matters of public security which didn't primarily involve him, and that his own personal peccadilloes need not become public if he were able to assist with their investigation. On receiving a signed statement concerning Meihua's disgraceful infidelities and Nigel's moral shortcomings, which Tubby conveniently recalled for the occasion, Gong congratulated him and thanked him for his commendable sense of civic duty as a benign foreigner.

*

On returning from his walk, Bucky had not wanted to surrender immediately and completely. He simply said they needed time to think and to talk about it all. The days that followed were calm but uncomfortable.

The following week, there was a knock at the door. It was Gong Anju and another man in uniform. They required Meihua to accompany them in order to discuss charges of adultery and immoral behaviour. Meihua was terrified, but Bucky remained calm.

'Is there any documentation concerning this?' he asked. 'Are we allowed to know who has made these claims?'

'At this moment, Mr Armitage, we are not required to tell you that. Your wife merely needs to answer our questions.'

Bucky remained calm. 'Are we allowed to know the detail of these charges? She can hardly defend herself if she doesn't know what she's charged with.'

'At this moment, sir, she isn't charged with anything. She just needs to answer our questions.'

'Look, I don't want to be rude, but my wife is pregnant and really not very well. Is it possible to discuss this here?'

Gong Anju cut in. 'I'm sorry, Mr Armitage. She will have to come with us. You will need to come and answer questions too.'

The other officer looked uncomfortable. He said something to Gong in a thick, impenetrable accent.

Gong relented. She asked Meihua, 'Can you tell us how you know Mr Nigel Ploughwright?'

'Yes, he's someone we met at the Shangri-La Hotel one night.'

'And can you tell us the nature of your relationship with Mr Ploughwright?'

'Yes, he's someone we met at the Shangri-La Hotel one night.'

'Do you have any other kind of relationship with Mr Ploughwright?'

'Yes, he briefly tried to teach me guitar.'

'And why did he stop?'

'Because it was clear to both of us that I have no talent.'

'Did you have any other kind of relationship with Mr Ploughwright?'

'No.'

'Listen –' interjected Bucky.

'Please, sir, if you'll just let us do our duty here.' The male officer was firm, but much less aggressive than Gong.

Gong continued, 'And can you tell us the nature of your relations with Mr Christopher Bligh?'

'Give us a break,' interrupted Bucky once again. 'She feels the same about Tubby as everyone else does. No one likes him much. He's a sleazy bastard.'

'I'm afraid, sir, if you're going to keep interrupting, we'll have to take you both away with us.'

There was a brief discussion, which Bucky didn't understand, and it was decided that they all needed to go to the station or the office or wherever people were taken when they needed to be taken.

Once there, the forces of justice decided to divide and conquer, so Meihua was taken to a room with Gong, and Bucky remained with the male officer. The officer sat down at a desk and hammered away at a typewriter for what seemed to be an eternity.

Gong went out and left Meihua to agonise. The smell of fear, sweat and urine hung in the air. The walls were very thin and she could hear clearly the male officer's typewriter next door and the conversation that ensued.

In the adjacent room, the officer looked up from his typewriter and asked Bucky, 'Can you tell us, sir, what you know about the relationship between your wife and Mr Ploughwright?'

'Yes. He briefly tried to teach my wife guitar…and failed.'

'Do you think he was attracted to her?'

'Probably. She's an attractive woman, don't you think?'

'I don't know anything about that, sir. I just know about the law… And what do you think your wife felt about him?'

'Revulsion.'

'Are you sure of that, sir?'

'Yes.'

'And what do you know about Mr Bligh?'

'I know he's a sleaze.'

'And what do you think your wife felt about –'

'Listen, I won't tell you what I think. I'll tell you what I know. Nigel Ploughwright and Tubby Bligh are both sleazy bastards. Everyone knows that. I'm sure they'd both like to jump my wife, and so would half the men she meets, but she's not the slightest bit interested. Nor is any other decent woman about town interested in them. Neither of these men had any opportunity and, if they say they have, it's just wishful thinking. Meihua is three months pregnant,' he said, lying slightly. 'It's my child,' he lied more blatantly, 'and half the time she's been sick as a dog and she's not in the mood for me, let alone a couple of sad hopefuls like them. So if you have any credible evidence from anyone respectable, drag it out and let's have a look at it.'

In the next room, Meihua heard every word clearly. Her heart was bursting simultaneously with shame for what she'd done and love for Bucky. She heard a noise, looked around, and realised that Gong had been there for some time and must have heard the whole thing. Gong looked quite grim.

Bucky continued, 'Have you got any credible witnesses apart from these two doubtful hopefuls? Isn't there supposed to be someone who complains about her behaviour or actions? If she's done what they say she's done, then they've got nothing to complain about. If she's been willing to go to bed with these men, then they won't want her locked away. They'd want to come back for more. These men are upset because they haven't been successful. Do you hear me complaining? If there's anyone in a position to complain, it's me. She's my wife, I love her, we have a child on the way, and these arseholes are just unhappy because they can't get their end in.'

Tears cascading down her cheeks, Meihua heard someone, presumably the other officer, get up and walk out of the room. Gong walked out of Meihua's room.

From their respective rooms, Bucky and Meihua listened intently to the conversation outside. At first, the two officers spoke in hushed tones, but gradually Gong's voice rose in volume and became more agitated. The other officer remained calm.

It seemed that Gong was not getting her way. She was not, however, likely to mention her own experience with Nigel as any sort of evidence or character reference, especially since she also was a married woman. Bucky and Meihua waited in their separate rooms for some half an hour, and then were allowed to wait together for another half hour, while different people had different conversations.

Finally, they were out on the street. The smell of stale piss and rotting garbage hovered in the grey sky of their Guilin paradise, but to Bucky and Meihua it smelt like freedom and looked like a new horizon. Meihua took his hand and it felt like the hand of someone who loved her. She listened to her heart and it sounded like a new song. She knew that the things that had mattered before were now not important. They had not brought her happiness. This man had.

In the end, everyone was happy. Apart from Bucky and Meihua, Tubby Bligh was also quite relieved. The story of forbidden lust that he had shared with Nigel did not need to be shared with his colleagues or anyone else. This was just as well, since he had been lying anyway. Gong Anju was happy because, after a little research, she was able to find other reasons to revoke Nigel Ploughwright's visa and have him deported. Nigel didn't particularly mind being deported because he was happy to seduce any woman anywhere. He could now plough fresh fields elsewhere.

The Tugboat Captain

Mr Payne was our grade seven teacher and we all liked him even though he was strict. He used to cane us regularly, but in those days we thought that was why we were sent to school.

When we wrote essays, he would often read some of the better efforts to the rest of the class. I was one of those whose work he sometimes read. This was a Good Thing in the eyes of my father, but a Bad Thing in the eyes of my classmates. Although I never wanted to incur the disapproval of my father, I didn't enjoy the ill will that my better efforts generated among my classmates.

On one occasion, being something of a smart-arse, I wrote a story about a tugboat captain, to whom I maliciously decided to give a completely unpronounceable Eastern European name. I had gleeful visions of Mr Payne tying himself in knots, trying to say this man's name. I felt this would be very jolly and worked conscientiously on the essay. It was successful.

'Alan Bailey,' he said, 'this is an excellent story. I think the class deserves to hear this.'

Oh yes, I thought. *Oh boy, oh joy!*

'Come out here and read it to the class.'

'I beg your pardon, sir?'

'Don't be shy, lad. Come out here and read your essay.'

Bugger. This wasn't supposed to happen.

Fortunately, I had a Plan B. I went to the front of the class and Mr Payne's face revealed nothing as he handed me my work. And so it was that I read my story about Captain S-z-m-y-s-c-z-k and his tugboat. However, when I reached the name in question, I read it as *Captain Smith*.

'Read that bit again, please, boy. I didn't hear you clearly.'

I reread the passage, pronouncing the name once again as *Captain Smith*.

'Come here, Bailey. Show me your work.'

Trepidation.

'What's this name here, boy?'

'Smith, sir. It's pronounced Smith.'

'Thank you for your assistance with that, Bailey. Stand in the corner. I'll deal with you in a moment.'

The class had to wait until lunchtime to find out why he had caned me.

The New Yorker

'Hi, Bazza. How ya doin'? Where's Tracy?'

'Not in her apartment, mate. I just got back from Washington Square and she's not home, so I thought I'd drop by and say g'day.'

'Hey, man, come in. I just brewed some coffee. Pixie! Can you make another cup of coffee, honey? Tracy's Austrian friend Bazza is here.'

'Australian…'

'Yeah, her Australian friend.'

'I gotta go, Conrad,' came a whining voice from the next room. 'My mom's at me for not doing my homework.' A young girl came in, buttoning up her shirt.

Pixie looked about thirteen, but Bazza was not taken aback. He had met her before, when he was visiting with his friend Tracy. Conrad supplied Tracy and most of her neighbours with dope or whatever.

'Hey, that's OK, gorgeous. You were great. Any chance you can come back later?'

'I dunno, Conrad. Mom's really down on me since she caught me with Brad.'

'Well, I wasn't that wild about Brad either, honey, but hey, me and your ma are good buddies.'

'You mean you supply her with smack.'

Conrad drew the young girl to him and slipped his hand down the back of her short shorts. 'You know I don't like you talkin' like that, Pixie. It ain't fittin' for a sweet young thing your age.'

'Conrad, it ain't fitting for a man your age to be all over his neighbour's daughter like a rash.'

Conrad was balding early, maybe in his late twenties. He was wearing low-cut jeans, cowboy boots and a loose-fitting tank top. He laughed, squeezed her left buttock and gave her a gentle shove towards the door. 'I'll see ya later, sweetie. Tell your ma I got that stuff for her.' He turned back to the table and finished rolling a three-paper joint. 'Here, try this. It'll clear your head,' he slurred.

Bazza took a single toke and gave it back.

'Naaah man, go again. Hang loose. This is New York.'

'*Exactamundo*, Conrad.' Bazza immediately felt self-conscious trying to ape this man's trendy-trendy speech. 'This is New York and I don't want to come unstuck in the street.'

'Hey, man, I gotta go out, see some friends, do some business. Come wit' me. It'll be an education. Don't worry. It's only a few blocks and you'll be wit' me. I'm a New Yorker.'

Conrad bustled around, looked in a cupboard and then went into a neighbouring room. He came back pushing an ancient shopping stroller, one of those enclosed canvas containers on wheels. Something that Granny Bunch might have pushed in the fifties or sixties.

'Hey, Cisco, *vamos!*' Bazza's entire repertoire of Spanish was derived from watching reruns of *The Cisco Kid*.

If the New Yorker had been a Californian, he would have had a cool Spanish reply, but he had to settle for, '*Yo, amigo*, tutti frutti.'

*

'Come in, darlings.' Barnaby was as cool as one could be in this, the age of disco: ocean blow-wave, striped boat-neck T-shirt, baggy white trousers turned up to mid-calf, canvas yachtie sneakers with no socks, gold chain that would have dragged him like a rock to the seabed.

His apartment was smooth too. Swedish furnishings throughout, interrupted periodically by hippie beanbags occupied by spaced out punters who were trying before buying. Hi-fi speakers resembling air raid bunkers, from which emanated the honeyed tones of Earl Klugh, playing 'Cast your Fate to the Wind'.

'I was expecting you, sweetheart. I've put a bag away for you somewhere. Come in the kitchen.'

It was a clean, white, modern kitchen, on one side of which there were wall-to-wall inbuilt cupboards. Barnaby started opening doors, looking for Conrad's purchase. Cupboard after cupboard revealed wheat-bag-sized plastic bags filled with marijuana.

'Most of this is local, darling, but I know you're a man of taste, so I've put some Acapulco Gold aside for you. Ah, here we are. This is yours. Come into the study. We can have a toke before you're on your way. Little bit tasted, little bit wasted. Yes, no? Does your gorgeous friend smoke, Conrad?'

Conrad's gorgeous friend Bazza was still hesitant about navigating New York with his feet in the street and his head in the clouds.

'It's his time of the week, man, so he's taking a holiday. Don't worry, though. He's cool.'

Bazza drifted back into the living room with the floaty boaties and lowered himself into a beanbag between the two speakers. Jay Berliner was backing George Benson's jazz version of 'California Dreaming' with some passionate flamenco guitar. Bazza didn't care how long Conrad and Barnaby were going to take.

*

Conrad eventually reappeared with his shopping stroller. He had been woozy when they arrived, but now he was starting to show some real wear and tear.

'Hang on, sweetie. You can't go out in the street like that.' Barnaby pointed out that the corners of Conrad's plastic bag were poking out the top of the trolley, revealing his contraband cargo. 'Here, use this.' Barnaby went back in the kitchen and reappeared with a tea towel, which he draped over Conrad's dope load. He tucked the corners in. 'There now. You're all shipshape.'

By this time, Bazza was light-headed from recycling the exhalations of the other tokers in the room. He levered himself out of the beanbag and reluctantly farewelled Barnaby and his music. He tried to shake his host's hand and, to his embarrassment, discovered that he didn't know the series of arcane grips and gestures necessary to maintain one's coolness.

Outside, Conrad slurringly consoled him. 'Hey, man, don't worry. He's got some strange moves. He's Californian.'

Bazza now understood why Barnaby had parted with 'Have a nice day' instead of the standard New York 'Take care'.

*

In the street, it became clear that Conrad was not only talking, but also walking with a slur. His difficulty maintaining a straight line was a concern, and Bazza was not really anxious to be caught walking through New York with a shopping stroller full of marijuana.

'Do you want me to take the trolley, mate?'

'No hassle, buddy. I do this every day. I'm a New Yorker.'

They navigated the streets wobblingly but successfully until Park Avenue. Then it became necessary to cross the road. The Australian thought the traffic resembled a high-speed logjam, but Conrad launched straight out into it. Bazza grabbed his arm and hauled him back on to the sidewalk.

'What's up, buddy? Whatcha doin'?'

'Hang on, mate. Just wait for a gap in the traffic. Let's not draw attention to ourselves.'

'Hey, Bazz. Just stick wit' me. I know what I'm doin'. I'm a New Yorker.' He wrenched himself free and once again, guided by his trolley, zigzagged out into the traffic.

Horns honked. Cars screeched to a halt. Drivers hurled abuse. Arms emerged from car windows and made immodest gestures.

The immodest gestures were reciprocated by Conrad. 'Blow it out your ass, buddy!'

Horrified, Bazza remained rooted to the sidewalk, hardly able to breathe. Even though very little surprises people in New York, he felt his companion was attracting attention.

Conrad had made it to the traffic island. He turned and exhorted Bazza. 'C'mon, man. It's OK. Ya just gotta stay cool.'

Then it happened. Encouraged by the absence of disaster, Conrad now attempted the second half of the crossing. He pushed his trolley off the island and into the roadway. There was a screeching of brakes and a very audible oath from within a vehicle. The car almost stopped in time, but Conrad's trolley was hurled back on to the island some five metres further on. Bazza stood aghast. Conrad stood stunned. Fortunately the stroller and its cargo had not burst open.

'Are you OK, Conrad?' Bazza yelled above the traffic noise.

None of the traffic had stopped. No reply. Conrad stood transfixed.

'Are you OK, Conrad?'

Still no reply. Conrad stood motionless.

Bazza mumbled an inarticulate prayer. 'Jesus, Conrad!'

The Australian stepped out into the roadway. More honking of horns, screeching of brakes, more obscenities and immodest gesticulation. Fuelled by adrenalin, Bazza reached the traffic island.

'For fuck's sake, Conrad! Are you OK?'

No reply. Conrad's eyes were glazed and he was trembling.

Bazz took off his denim jacket and draped it over Conrad's shoulders. 'Stay here. I'll be back.'

He raced along the island and picked up the trolley. Its precious contents were still intact, although the tea towel needed relocation. One of the wheels was quite wibbly-wobbly. Bazza quickly realised that it was easier to drag the stroller behind than to push it in front.

Conrad was still shivering and dribbling. He stammered something about not getting the car's number and the stroller not being insured. Bazza removed the jacket from Conrad's trembling shoulders, used it to wipe away the slobber and then helped pour him back into the jacket.

'Come on, mate. Let's get out of here before we attract any more attention.' He realised, though, that very few people had cared, stopped or even noticed.

He grasped Conrad by the jacket sleeve and, this time, waited for a gap in the traffic. Dragging the trolley with one hand and Conrad with the other, he successfully negotiated the rest of the crossing. He had not anticipated spending his afternoon wheeling a wobbly shopping trolley, filled with Acapulco Gold, through the streets of New York.

'No hassle, buddy,' dribbled Conrad. 'Just stick wit' me. I'm a New Yorker.'

Country Life

Michael Wells was a young bank clerk who had been posted to Burra in the country. He chose to live forty kilometres away in a small house just out of Manoora. The house dated from the days when farmers could afford to employ and lodge seasonal workers. The landlord was now pleased to have someone living there. Otherwise, the local lads would be taking their girlfriends there for 'hooking' parties and the house would quickly be ruined. Consequently, the rent was very cheap.

It was a beautiful setting with softly sloping plains, sheltered here and there by shade gums for the sheep. The farmer lived a kilometre away and the nearest house was visible, but across the road and three or four hundred metres away. Michael knew it was the home of Harry Barlow and his wife, but in all the time he lived there, he never saw either of them.

Michael's life burst into Technicolor when two young women, Helena and Millie, arrived at his door and wanted to stay a while. He had met them at a party in the city a few months earlier and forgotten about them, but it seemed they had not forgotten him. It was probably not so much the thought of Michael that fired their collective imagination as the opportunity to live in a small house in the country. After all, it was the early seventies.

Whatever their reasons, Michael's self-appointed guests quickly settled into country life and all three became quite attached to each other, enthusiastically and energetically, especially in the evenings. The women enjoyed the privacy of isolation. In the mornings, they would go out to the long-drop toilet, sometimes partly, sometimes completely unclothed. Initially, they were not aware at what time devout church warden Sean Hanrahan would be driving past in a fully laden school bus. Michael later learned from the local pub that the bus had nearly rolled over sideways when twenty-three local children had all raced to one side of the bus to gawk at Millie.

Despite the exhaustion in the mornings, this *ménage à trois* may sound like heaven to most young men and, in many ways, it was. However, it was not without its complications. After several months, it became clear that Michael's feelings were stronger for Helena, and he was clearly paying her more attention.

With only the three of them in the house, it was difficult to pretend that this was not happening. It was embarrassing and eventually a frank discussion became unavoidable. This kind of discussion is never easy, but there was no anger. There were no recriminations. A few tears were shed. They all hugged each other and made farewell love. The next day, Millie caught the train back to Adelaide.

Helena stayed with Michael for another year, even moving to another country property closer to Adelaide. Michael had been posted to another town. It was some time before Michael realised that Helena had only lived with him to make her previous lover jealous. In the end, her strategy was successful and she went back to him. Life can be like that.

*

One fine day, forty-two years later, Michael took a long-time friend for a day trip. He thought it would be a pleasant day to drive to Manoora in the morning, have lunch at the Mintaro pub and visit Martindale Hall in the afternoon. A sort of historical tour of his youth.

Arriving in Manoora, he realised nothing had really changed. He remembered how country people were always aware of strangers in the district, so he thought it would be polite to drop by at the neighbouring house, still standing some three or four hundred metres from his former dwelling. He turned off the road and drove up the long dirt track to the house.

'Hello?' He knocked at the front door and called several times.

It was a long wait. Finally, an old man, breathing heavily, still in dressing gown and slippers, limped to the door. It occurred to Michael that it might be the same man who lived there back then.

'G'day. My name's Michael Wells. I used to live in the old house across the road. I was just passing by with a friend and I thought we might stop and have a look.'

'Oh.'

'I just thought I should drop by and say who we are and what we're doing so no one will think we're prowlers.'

The man peered through the wire screen door. 'You say you used to live there?'

'Oh yeah. Quite some time ago. I doubt if anyone around here would remember now.'

'When did you live there?'

'Oh, a long time ago now. Back in 1972.'

'Tst!' the old man tutted. 'The two women…'

A Manly Man

Mr Burke liked to drink. It was the manly thing to do: just beer, not spirits or wanky wines. His friends were all manly friends. They liked football and golf and horse-racing… oh, and drinking beer. They were the things that made them manly.

I forgot to mention that Mr Burke was a teacher, which was nowhere near as manly, but he made up for it with his leisure-time pursuits. He was a good teacher, although at times quite scary. He felt that this was traditional and, incidentally, the manly way to be. His ability to instil what he saw as a healthy dose of anxiety and apprehension into his students ensured that he always had their complete attention. They didn't dare not learn. Their good results in examinations assured him of the respect of staff and students alike.

All was going well for Mr B, as his students called him, until one weekend, driving home at three o'clock in the morning, he turned his old Ford upside down when it failed to follow his command on a sharp bend. This was inconvenient to say the least, as his car was a total write-off.

Although Mr B was not written off, help was needed to extract him from the remains of his car. Police were called, and an ambulance, and he was carted off to hospital. This was more inconvenient for him than the loss of his car, as the doctors and subsequently the police discovered he had a large quantity of blood in his alcohol stream.

One thing followed another. Mr Burke was summoned to appear in court and explain himself. His explanations were deemed unsatisfactory and the judge deprived him of his driver's licence for twelve months. This was not entirely inconvenient as he no longer had a car. His friends laughed a loud, manly laugh, slapped him on the back and drove him to work for a year.

Time and a half passed by, and Mr Burke was promoted to senior master in another school. By this time, he had his licence back and he thought it fitting that he have a better car than previously, one that was more appropriate to his higher station in life. He bought a second-hand Mercedes.

However, in recent times Mr B's attitude to life had hardened somewhat. He felt that the cruel blow dealt to him by fate and his harsh treatment in court had not been fully justified, and an element of bitterness now tainted his manliness. Whereas he had previously been accepted and respected for his firm but fair control in the classroom, he was now seen by his new students as domineering and unnecessarily strict. He was not loved.

One day, he was teaching a senior maths class when a student came knocking at the door. Mr Burke was not pleased. It was ten minutes before lunch break and he was writing the solution to a problem on the whiteboard.

'Go away! Come back at the end of the lesson.' He continued writing.

The student hesitated at the door for some seconds, raised his hand to knock again, thought better of it and went away.

Some minutes later, more knocking. There was a glass pane in the door, so Mr Burke and those at the front of the class could see it was a different boy. The first student hadn't dared come back. The teacher ignored this second interruption. The boy knocked again.

'Go away, boy! Come back at the end of the lesson.'

Hesitation. 'But, sir –'

'Do you hear me, boy? Go away!'

The student went away.

There was a further brief period of Mr B casting his pearls before the class, and then…another knock at the door.

The maths teacher was furious. 'Do you hear –' He stopped abruptly.

The principal didn't wait for Mr Burke's invitation. He opened the door and walked straight in.

'Mr Burke, I'll look after your class for you. I think you'd better go to the staff car park. Your Mercedes is on fire.'

Where There's a Will

My name is Fredrick Handel-Marney. I have been a lawyer for twenty-seven years now. The reading of a family member's will is a dramatic cinema tradition that very seldom occurs in real life. Sometimes, however, it happens that the deceased has requested this gathering of those involved, often for the sake of having a last say. On these occasions, I confess, I am often appalled by the unctuous hypocrisy, barely concealed self-interest and, at times, naked greed of those present.

In particular, I retain vivid memories of the following colourful encounter.

On the day I read the will, two of the daughters, Michelle and Rachel, arrived early. While I was sorting through the various files on my desk, one of the girls leaned across to the other.

'So how much money was there?'

'Give it a rest, Rachel,' Michelle said. 'There isn't any money. She spent it all on the trip to Fiji and then that wanky trip of "self-discovery" in Germany.'

'She didn't discover herself, Michelle. She lost herself. She totally forgot she had family to look after.'

'I don't think she lost anything. She drank it all.'

'So why are we here? The beach house?'

'Beach house? It's just a hovel in the middle of the mangroves.'

The drone of the traffic outside became louder and a short, stocky man appeared at the open door.

'Whoa, shut up! It's Matthew… Dad, what are you doing here?'

'I'm your father, aren't I, Rachel?'

'Yes, but –'

'I was Florence's husband, wasn't I?'

'Once upon a time, but what makes you think you're going to get anything?'

Matthew rolled his eyes. 'Oh, you're such a sweet young thing! Well, strangely enough, I've got this letter inviting me to be here today. How about you guys?'

'We're her daughters, Matthew,' replied Michelle.

'Well, you may find this strange, but Florence and I actually chose each other and cared for each other somewhere back there. We didn't choose you. You just happened. So, have you actually cared for anyone?'

The question had probably never occurred to Rachel before and didn't seem to interest her now. 'You're such a bastard, Matthew.'

'I love you too, dear.' Matthew picked up an adjacent chair and moved it several metres to the rear so he could see all before him. 'Where's Priscilla?' he asked.

At that moment, a well groomed man in an expensive three-piece suit entered the room. He immediately approached me and introduced himself as J. Henry Wiley LLB, employed to represent the interests of the first-born daughter, Ms Priscilla Weston, born of a previous partner. Ms Weston could not be present. She had important business to deal with in Rome.

The two young women exchanged scornful glances.

Michelle leaned across to Rachel and whispered, 'Wanker!'

It was uncertain whether this referred to Priscilla or her lawyer, but the two women ignored the two men and quietly continued their savagery.

'Well, the beach house must be worth something. We can just sell it straight away.'

'But who'd buy it? Who'd want to live there? It's such a backwater swamp for redneck bogans. And the house is just so crap.'

Mr Wiley didn't wait to be introduced. 'Ah well, I actually have instructions in relation to the St Kilda beach property. Ms Weston has the business acumen and wherewithal to exploit the property. The dwelling can be bulldozed to maximise the value of the land and a contract can be formulated whereby the other parties can share some percentage of income derived from the development.'

Matthew interrupted, 'Forget it.'

The newcomer persisted, 'I believe there is still an outstanding mortgage on the property. My client's stepfather, Mr Matthew Harrison, and my client may have the combined resources to pay off the mortgage.'

Matthew was definitely not interested. He didn't have the money. He didn't want the property. Priscilla was the daughter of some other man. He didn't like her and he didn't trust her.

'The house is too far away and nobody would want to live in it,' Matthew said. 'And I'm not interested in the swamp around it. It's downwind from a sewage treatment plant. She can buy my share if she wants.'

'What share?' Matthew's daughters were not interested in the newcomer's suggestion and even less interested in their father's opinion. 'Just sell it and share the money three ways.'

'What do you mean, three ways?' asked Matthew.

'Her daughters, of course,' said Rachel. 'You never gave a rat's about us.'

'Isn't her German toy boy living there at present? asked Michelle.

'Bugger him. He can rack off,' replied Rachel.

'You reckon? I'll bet he's got his sights on some of her goodies. He was in it for more than the shagging.'

'Where is he? Is he coming today?'

'He's already here,' came a voice from the back of the room. There was a man standing behind Matthew. 'Florence said her daughters were like this.'

'What would she know?' snapped Rachel. 'She was just our…' She stopped abruptly, realising she was about to say something silly.

I felt that things were getting a bit out of hand and, as presiding lawyer, it fell to me to maintain some semblance of decorum. 'You, sir,' I addressed our latest arrival, 'must be Ms Harrison's friend or partner from Germany?'

'Correct.' he replied with hardly any accent. 'I am her German toy boy.'

I tried not to smile. 'Ah, Mr Jens von der Witt. Well then, it would appear that we're all here. Shall we begin?' I was not, of course, asking anyone. It was time to finish the family circus and begin the reading of the will. I unfolded the document and read aloud.

'This is the last Will and Testament of me, Florence Harrison of Backwater Road, St Kilda in the state of South Australia, home duties.

'1. I revoke all former Wills and Codicils and declare this to be my last Will and Testament.

'2. I appoint my lawyer, Mr Fredrick Handel-Marney (hereafter referred to as "my Trustee") as sole Executor and Trustee of this Will.

'3. I direct my Trustee to pay and satisfy all my debts and expenses as soon as possible after my death.

'4. I declare that my Trustee will have the power to sell any asset by either public auction or private contract for such price and on such terms as he thinks fit, at his sole discretion.'

'Get on with it!' came a female voice from the group.

I continued. '5. I bequeath the remainder of my estate not otherwise disposed of by this Will to my current partner, Mr Jens von der Witt, currently of St Kilda, South Australia.'

Loud discontent from the entire family.

I continued stoically. '6. To my ex-husband, Matthew Harrison, whom I promised to mention in my will: Hello, Matthew! Furthermore, I desire that my body be left to Matthew Harrison because things have been a bit slow for him lately.'

Chortling and tittering, presumably from all except Mr Harrison.

I continued. 'In addition, I bequeath to Matthew Harrison $250 on the condition that he remarry. In this way, since my daughters won't regret my death, there will be at least one woman who will.

'7. To my daughters, namely Priscilla, Michelle and Rachel, I leave $1 each for the kindness and love they have never shown me. Furthermore, I bequeath another $30 in order to buy them a book about good manners.'

'Very funny!'

I ignored the interruption and continued. '8. In witness whereof I have hereunto set my hand this 13th day of blah blah blah, yada yada yada.'

There was a stunned silence. Then those present managed to express themselves.

'The bastard!'

'The bitch!'

'What a complete arsehole!'

Mr von der Witt felt obliged to say something on her behalf. 'I don't think we're being completely fair here. Don't you feel we need to show some respect for the dead?'

As these rather uncharitable utterances were being expressed in my chambers, I also felt obliged to establish some semblance of decency. 'Ladies and gentlemen, I know we can all feel a little upset by the demise a loved one, but –'

'Fucking loved one! Fucking bullshit!'

I struggled on gallantly. 'If we can just calm down, we can perhaps have a look at the financial statements, so we have a better idea what all this might mean.'

Michelle offered her own financial analysis. 'It means we've been frauded, dickhead.'

Mr von der Witt once again came to my aid. 'I think we shouldn't jump to conclusions here. Let's just allow the gentleman to finish.'

'Thank you, Mr von der Witt. Could we just wait a moment and see to what extent the wishes of the deceased party could be carried out?'

Gradually the outrage subsided and the lynch mob became attentive.

'Thank you. You are, of course, aware that most of the deceased party's liquid assets were spent on trips to Fiji and Germany, the majority of the expenditure being for fares, accommodation, car rental, food, alcohol and other local travel. There was also a motor vehicle that was sold in Australia prior to the German trip in order to free up cash flow. That money became part of expenditure during the trip.

'On the property at St Kilda, there was a mortgage that had fallen some six months in arrears. The house and property needed to be sold off to cover outstanding debts. This left the estate free of debt, although there was very little money left to satisfy the wishes of Ms Harrison. Unfortunately, Mr von der Witt will not be able to inherit the house and property, nor can we find the $250 to encourage Mr Harrison to remarry. However, we can find the $33 for the three daughters and their book on good manners.'

'Bloody lawyers!' snapped Matthew.

'Please, Mr Harrison.' Now it was Mr Wiley coming to the rescue. 'Abuse is not at all helpful. May I ask, Mr Handel-Marney, what did you get for the house and property?'

'Well, we were very lucky to pay off outstanding accounts, but we were able to write off the mortgage and all other debts.'

Mr Wiley persisted. 'And how much money was involved?'

'Well, indeed, the property and especially the house were in very poor condition and we were lucky to get $75,000 for them.'

There was a stunned silence in the room.

Now, Mr Wiley became quite tasteless in his pursuit of pointless information. 'And are we able to know who the buyer was?'

'Really, Mr Wiley, it was very difficult to find a buyer at all in the current market.'

'So who bought it?' Matthew Harrison insisted.

'Well, under the circumstances, I felt obliged to offer assistance, so my wife bought it.'

I Love You, Daddy

Alana stood under the shower, the water drumming on her head, neck and shoulders. It ran caressingly down her back and chest, but modestly formed a delta around her young, boyish nipples. She considered her body too firm, too muscular. The men she had known all seemed to move south from her breasts too quickly. Alana was thinking about Eva.

Eva was a doe-eyed creature whose svelte, graceful body and olive skin were unlike Alana's athletic figure but anaemic complexion. Unlike the men Alana had known, Eva lingered long and lovingly before moving on to other mysteries. She always seemed to get joy in giving pleasure, rather than taking it for herself.

Today, Alana spent longer than usual in the shower. It was an important day. She was going to meet her father for the first time. She still had doubts whether this was a good idea.

Her father was yet another man who had fled his responsibilities. He had shared a few moments of happiness with her mother, Felicity, or maybe it was just he who had enjoyed the moments. When he had discovered Felicity was pregnant, he had disappeared, leaving her to raise Alana. He had made no offers of help. Later, when he realised Felicity was not pursuing him for maintenance, he had come back to his hometown, but had never sought her out. He had never tried to find out whether the child was a son or a daughter, had never sent her a birthday present, had never come to watch her play soccer.

After years of equivocating, Alana had waded through all the bureaucracy, located him, written to him and phoned him. She was aware she might regret this and she would have to put up with him for the rest of his life. She had tormented herself with these questions for a long time. So today, why was her heart thumping? Why were tears welling up in her eyes as she drove across town? What would he look like? Should she hug him? Should she kiss him? What would they say? Should she come straight out and ask why he had never cared enough?

There was a screech of brakes. Alana realised it was the sound of her own tyres. A dog had run on the road and her reaction had been automatic. She had driven halfway across town in this absent-minded fashion, but remembered nothing of it. She bit her lip and concentrated on the road. If she didn't pay attention to what was happening around her, she might not get there.

She knew in advance what the neighbourhood would look like. She had lived in this town all her life. She knew that, living in this area, he was wealthy. This suburb reflected the comfort and the lifestyle that he had been unwilling to share with her mother.

Eventually, Alana was there. Not all the dwellings were obviously numbered, so she was counting the houses as she drove slowly down the street. This must be his house. There may have been a number on the gatepost, but it was hidden by a very thick, very high hedge. Although the gate was open, she didn't drive in. Her car was not a recent model and was rather dilapidated. It wasn't that she was too ashamed for him to see. She wanted the neighbours to know that someone from the other side of town was visiting him. She locked her car, although she was sure that no one around here would want to steal it.

Alana walked through the gate and started up a long gravel drive that arced around to the front of the house. Another branch of the drive went straight on past the house and twenty metres further ended at a three-door garage. In front of one of these doors was a recent model Mercedes.

For just a moment, she wondered if she should go to the back door, but quickly dismissed the idea. She was his daughter. She would not go to the tradesman's entrance. The garden was geometrical and carefully manicured, as was the vast central lawn. There were roses in abundance and she wondered if it was her father who tended them, or did he have a gardener? The side fences, like the front hedge, guarded the owner's privacy. This was probably not particular to her father's property. She imagined all residents in the neighbourhood guarded their privacy jealously. She looked for signs of children, but there were none.

The house was large and conservative, from the first half of the twentieth century: one of those with the pseudo towers on the front corners to give it a sense of grandeur. For a moment, Alana wondered what was in the towers. Was there a staircase? Could one ascend to the battlements to get an early view of those approaching? The two sides of the house that she could see had a well shaded veranda.

She knocked on the front door and waited. No one came. She discovered a doorbell and pressed it. She heard nothing. Perhaps it didn't work, or perhaps the door and walls were very thick. Maybe the bell sounded further inside the house. Perhaps his wife would answer the door. He had said he was married, but that his wife would be out. Maybe Alana should have brought a friend. Maybe she should turn around and go home. The door opened.

'Alana?' He was short and wiry with an engaging smile and a mop of stylishly careless hair. A Bermuda jacket suggested he had made a special effort for the occasion.

'Bernie?' She knew from all the bureaucracy that his name was Bernard and he had told her on the phone she should call him Bernie. She had practised this moment over and over in her head and in her heart, but when the moment came, her voice broke.

It didn't matter. He stepped forward and embraced her, and she remained speechless. She knew the words she wanted to say, but they wouldn't come out. Tears poured down her cheeks and her body began to shake convulsively. She was not sure what this meant. It was not love. It may have been anger. It may have been confusion. Maybe it was relief from the endless yearning that had racked her heart and mind for years. She was angry because she had not wanted to cry. She knew she was crying for herself, and didn't want him to think she was crying for him.

'Alana,' he whispered gently.

They embraced in the doorway for some time until gradually her shaking subsided.

'Come in, come in. Come through into the drawing room. Would you like tea or coffee, or maybe a beer or wine or some champagne?'

She followed him into a tastefully decorated salon and sat on a red velvet sofa, a perfect match for the curtains, although not currently fashionable. She would have liked a drink, but then he would have to organise it, which would only prolong the agonising silence. 'No, I'm fine, thanks.'

'So what have you been doing all this time?' he asked.

There was an awkward silence, and then they both laughed at the silliness of the question. She told him about her studies and her job. She told him about her mother, although he hadn't asked. She told him about her relationship with Eva and how they had moved in together.

'But you're a good-looking girl. Why don't you have a boyfriend?'

'Because I've got a beautiful girlfriend that I love dearly,' Alana snapped back.

'Hey, sorry. I didn't mean to offend.'

'Well, you did.'

'Hey, look, I said I was sorry.'

Alana wondered if she should leave politely before too many bridges were burnt. She was not overwhelmed by a desire for reconciliation, but she needed time to think. She stayed another half hour making polite conversation, and then excused herself.

*

'I have some wine we need to drink. Can I come over tomorrow for a private chat?'

Alana's text message on the previous day had been simple, and now she was here at the door. The weather was fine, so Alana was wearing a short denim skirt and a thin cheesecloth shirt, a jacket slung casually across her shoulder. Beneath the shirt she wore no undergarment and she could tell this made Bernie uncomfortable.

'Hey, if I'd known you were going to dress up, I'd have worn a suit and tie.'

Alana let his awkward attempt at humour pass and breezed through the door. She didn't wait to be ushered into the lounge.

'Glasses,' she called back over her shoulder. 'We need brandy balloons.'

'I thought we were drinking wine.'

'We were, but I drank that last night with Eva.'

Bernie came in and put two brandy balloons on the coffee table.

'What kind of music would you like?' he asked. 'It's over there. Choose anything you like.'

He looked a little surprised when she chose a Palestrina Mass, but said nothing. Alana had opened the bottle and poured the brandy, perhaps a little too generously, but Bernie didn't complain.

They sat at opposite ends of the sofa and talked about the music. It seemed that they had similarly eclectic tastes, so they toasted Palestrina. They talked about Alana's studies and her job. Bernie congratulated her and they toasted her achievements. Bernie talked about his job. They toasted his success. They talked about Alana's hopes for the future and Bernie had suggestions and advice. They toasted Alana's future. Alana admired his house and furnishings and they toasted Bernie's good taste. Bernie complimented Alana on her choice of brandy and she facetiously complimented him on his knowledge of good brandies. They toasted their good taste.

By this stage, they were both extremely jolly, but it was clear that Bernie had done too much tasting and toasting. He had been draining his glass each time while Alana had just been sipping.

He returned to his concern for Alana's personal life. 'So how long have you known Eva?'

'About eighteen months. We've been living together for about a year now.'

'Did you know any guys before that?'

'Quite a few, but they were all jerks.'

'What do you mean, jerks?'

'Well, just that. They were jerks. They were just interested in kicking a goal and moving on.'

'Yes, but young guys can be like that. A girl doesn't need to come across. You just have to be patient until you find the right fellow comes along.'

'I don't need to find the right man. I've found the right woman.'

'OK, so this is something that makes you happy right now, but don't you think in the long run you're going to be happier with a man?'

'No.'

'Well, that's what I'm saying. I mean, that's how you feel at present, but so far as a long-term, ongoing relationship is concerned, don't you feel you're going to get more out of life with a man?'

'No.'

Bernie blundered on, 'I mean like, when I was young, I was probably very certain of myself too, and very fixed in my attitudes, but we all change as we grow older.'

'How come you weren't more fixed in your attitude towards my mother? How come you didn't stay with her?'

Bernie squirmed. 'Oh, look, Alana, that was different. We were both very young and it wouldn't have worked. And I certainly didn't know you were going to be born,' he lied.

'Would it have made a difference?'

'Of course. I wouldn't have walked away from my responsibilities.'

'So you didn't love her?' Alana continued. 'You just wanted to kick a goal?'

'Alana, it wasn't like that. They were different times.'

'Mum said she didn't mind too much.'

Bernie looked relieved. She was letting him off the hook.

Alana continued, 'She said you were no sooner in than you came, and that you were no sooner come than you were gone.'

Bernie's jaw dropped.

'But then,' she continued, 'like you say, young guys can be like that. I suppose you're going to say you're a better lover now.'

Bernie had nowhere to go. This was totally uncharted territory for him, and the brandy wasn't helping. He was obviously not in any condition to have this kind of conversation with a daughter, particularly with a newly discovered daughter.

Alana moved closer on the sofa. She put her hand on his thigh. 'I mean, you're saying that I should be more interested in men, but young men can be unreliable for either short-term or long-term satisfaction. Do you think older men are going to be any better? I mean, don't feel bad, but it's probably better to come early than to not be able to get there at all?'

'Alana, I –'

'Hey, I don't mean you, Bernie. I mean like, generally speaking… Anyway, I mean, you're way too old –'

'You might think so, princess,' he hissed, 'but everything is still in working order.'

'I bet you say that to all the women,' she teased.

'No, darling, just to you.' Bernie was way too drunk for this game of chess and Alana had him in check. If he'd had the willpower, he could have resisted her checkmate, but the truth was, he was only too willing to be mated. She laughed and squeezed his thigh.

Bernie was lost. He turned and pulled her to him, slipping his hand inside her cheesecloth shirt and grasping her cool, white breast. She put her arms around him and kissed him, her hands wrenching his shirt tails from his trousers. She sank back into the sofa, allowing his kiss to slip down to her now naked breast. She tore his shirt open, buttons flying everywhere, and tore at his chest with her fingernails.

'Ow, you bitch,' he grunted. 'I'll show you what it's like with a real man.'

The rest was history. However, unlike those heaving, panting cinema epics, it was a very brief story: no more than two minutes and he was spent. Alana feigned pleasure, but was relieved when he rolled off and lay beside her on the floor.

She put her head on his bloody chest and fondled the soggy remains of his supposed virility. Blood on her face, she gently kissed his chest, lay her head back on his shoulder, and sank into silence. 'That was so good,' she said as he drifted away, partly from satisfaction, partly from intoxication, into a deep sleep.

Alana, however, was not asleep. She stood up, took the nearly empty bottle of brandy by the neck and hit Bernie over the head with it. The bottle broke, staining the carpet with a mixture of blood and brandy. She then ripped her cheesecloth shirt open from its V-neck to her waist. She punched herself on the fleshy inside of her forearm and twice in the face, once on the cheek and once on the mouth. She checked in the wall mirror and was pleased to see this blow to her mouth had split her lip and drawn blood. She went back to Bernie and wiped her bleeding lip on his knuckles and his semen on her face.

Alana phoned the police emergency number, gave the address and reported a rape. It hadn't been her intention to hit him so hard, but she didn't want him to regain consciousness before the police arrived. On the other hand, he needed to be alive to face the consequences of his previous and current, real and supposed actions. Sometimes, she told herself, the law needs help to ensure that justice is done.

A Silly Question

In my heart, Aunt Mary was a hero. In a family that hypocritically called itself both Protestant and Christian, she had, in her teens, dared to become Catholic. With the exception of her mother, who had an Irish Catholic background, the entire family opposed her conversion. This was well before I was born, but forty years later, they were still making snide comments about it.

My mother died when I was young and my father, Fred, lived in fear that Mary would spirit me away and have me converted to Catholicism. On one occasion, she took me out for a drive on a Saturday afternoon. Some convent at Glenelg was having a fete. I always loved going for a drive with Auntie Mary, but the fete itself was boring; lots of being introduced to nuns as her nephew Angus. Being hugged and kissed by nuns had very limited charm. Anyway, when we got back, Mary copped hell from Fred for taking me to a convent. I remember he had hold of her finger and he was twisting it.

'Fred, you're hurting me!' she said, but he didn't stop.

I remember seeing afterwards and knowing that her finger didn't look right. At that stage, I didn't know the word 'dislocate'. I wasn't allowed to accompany her to the doctor's.

Mary was like a mother to me. She was there for me as much as Fred would allow and we were always laughing and going places together. Though our beliefs were not the same and we subsequently lived our lives very differently, I was never in doubt about her unconditional love. She was the only bead in my family rosary.

It had fallen to her, the youngest daughter in the family and unmarried, to care for her ageing mother for more than twenty-five years, thus surrendering any hope of marital happiness. It was well before the times when unmarital happiness was acceptable. Mary was no great beauty, but she had a delightful personality. She almost certainly could have made some man very happy if the rest of the family had not abandoned to her the responsibility for their mother.

*

Many years later, Mary was in Melbourne for the wedding of some distant relative's daughter. You must excuse my vagueness on this issue because, apart from Mary, very few people in the family knew or cared who was who.

At the reception, Mary, by then in her early eighties, was outside on the balcony, quietly sipping a shandy. Someone called Alex, beer in hand, stepped out on to the balcony to enjoy the evening air and, seeing Mary, thought it would be polite to sit with her and make small talk. At a certain point, he must have felt their conversation too trivial and boldly launched into something a little deeper.

'How come you never got married, Mary?'

Mary's expression revealed nothing. 'No one ever asked me, Alex.'

Alex stared deep into his beer for maybe half a minute, drained it and stood up, mumbling something about needing a refill.

Cheerfully recounting the story to me some years later, Mary said, 'Well, it was a damned silly question, wasn't it? I wasn't going to let him off lightly.'

Relationship... Relationship...

The English tourist started yelling at Chen and poking him in the chest. Chen looked around. People were turning and looking at them and there was a policeman at the corner of the street. The policeman noticed and started to walk towards them.

The young Chinese man knew foreigners could get away with almost anything if the police understood what they were saying. The authorities supported them because the government didn't want any bad international press regarding foreigners. They were a protected species.

Chen could have made a run for it, but he looked again at the Englishman's expensive suit and watch. The man had money and plenty of it. Chen seized a single finger and twisted it violently up behind the tourist's back, causing him to bend forward. The foreigner let out a loud yelp, but the people around them paid no attention. The man was a tourist and they weren't going to take sides against a fellow local.

Chen frogmarched the stranger into an adjacent alleyway, keeping the finger twisted to breaking point and putting his hand over his prisoner's mouth. Halfway down the alley it was dark and secluded. Chen took the man's watch and quickly rummaged through his pockets. Almost no money. There was a card wallet. He flipped it open. A cascade of credit cards concertinaed out. The man's name was Simon Lawson. Chen scowled and put the cards in his pocket. They were not really what he had wanted, but he needed time to think. At the other end of the alley was the Li River. Chen pushed the foreigner towards it.

They burst out of the alley on to the levee. Chen's younger brother Dawei was out on the river, supposedly fishing, and immediately saw them. Other older fishermen saw them too, but continued fishing.

It wasn't their business. Dawei punted over to the shore and the two brothers loaded their treasure on to the bamboo raft. The man was making muffled, gagging noises, so Dawei rammed a small, dead fish into his mouth. Chen laid the man flat on his face on the raft so he was less visible, and sat on him.

'*Why did you bring him, Brother?*' Chen's brother snapped in Chinese. The Englishman didn't understand a word. '*You were just supposed to grab his money and dump him.*'

'*He hasn't got much money on him. Just this wallet of credit cards.*'

'*We don't want to mess about with that kind of thing. It's too dangerous.*'

'*Shut up, Little Brother! Let's get out of here.*'

The brother put down his pole, picked up the hand-held outboard motor lying on the deck and started it. Tourists love to photograph the old fishermen with their pointy hats and their captive fishing birds, punting their bamboo rafts on the Li River, but why would you propel yourself with a pole when you can use a petrol-driven motor? The noise of the motor covered any fishy grunting and muffled shouting from their victim.

Fifteen minutes downstream, they were in a rusty corrugated-iron cabin. Their captive was sitting more comfortably, but bound and gagged, on the dirt floor.

Chen reverted to English. 'So, Simon Lawson, where your hotel?'

'Yangshuo Green Lotus Hotel. I can take you there.'

'No, you can't. We know where is Green Lotus Hotel. Where is your electronic door card?'

'It's in that card wallet. Take me with you. You won't find the money. You need to take me with you.'

'If there is money, we find it, but there is no door card in wallet. Where is your door card?'

'I don't know, honestly. It should be in that wallet. Just tell them at the front desk that you've lost it. They'll let you in.'

'You think we are fool? We are Chinese and room is booked to foreigner.'

Dawei drew Chen aside and suggested in Chinese that the door card might have fallen out in the alley. They could go back and look for it.

'*No way,*' Chen replied. '*He's not carrying much money, so probably there's not much in his hotel room.*' Chen drew the fishing knife from his brother's belt. '*But we have his cards. I think we can persuade him to give us the passwords for these.*'

*

Dawei guarded the prisoner while Chen went back to Yangshuo and tried the cards in a variety of ATMs. Most of the passwords worked, but there were limits on withdrawal. The money he took out was princely in China, but could have been so much more. Chen went back to the cabin to share the money with Dawei and discuss what they might do. He could always go back the next day and withdraw more money. He once again seized his younger brother's knife, held it to the foreigner's throat and asked him about the passwords that had not been successful.

'Some of those cards have expired if you look at the date on them. And my company is not always as successful as either of us might hope. I can't guarantee that all the accounts have money in them.'

'Then maybe you dead soon, my friend.'

Simon Lawson looked squarely into Chen's eyes. 'Listen, most of those cards and most of that money isn't mine. It all belongs to my company. If you keep withdrawing the daily limit from those accounts for a few days, they'll realise and block withdrawals.'

'Then we kill you.'

'Do you really think they'll care? They'll just notify the police in Yangshuo and the Yangshuo police will check the surveillance video at the banks where you've withdrawn the money. Yangshuo is not a big town. You'll be recognised.'

The two brothers had hoped he would feel more threatened.

'Listen,' he continued. 'You may feel quite pleased about the money you have so far, but it's not going to last all that long. I can offer you the opportunity to build a better future. You can earn a lot more money for a longer time. Your honesty doesn't matter to me 'cause it's not my money, and it won't matter much to my company because they're not very honest either.'

'What you mean?' Dawei snapped. 'Why we trust you?'

Chen calmed his brother down. The foreigner clearly had some kind of proposition. It would be foolish not to give him a hearing.

'I've been sent here to establish a tourism business in China,' Lawson continued. 'The company will need local agents and employees, people who know the region and local law and officials. We can offer you and your family jobs that will last all your lives.'

Chen realised his brother's question was not silly. 'So why we trust you?'

'Because we need people like you. I know bugger all about this place.'

'Bugger all?'

'Nothing. I know nothing about this area, except that it's crawling with tourist suckers.'

'Crawling with two suckers?'

Lawson explained, 'There are lots of dumb tourists.'

'Just like you,' Dawei snapped.

'*Shut up, Little Brother.* So, Englishman, how you think we can help you?'

Lawson explained they needed someone who could make contacts with the local community, with businesses, with hotels, with restaurants, with transport, with banks, with Chinese authorities and guides. 'We can talk about it,' he said. 'I don't suppose you have a suit? Doesn't matter. We can buy you some.'

'You do this for us?' asked Dawei.

'Not just for you. For me. For the company. We can help each other. Do you want the job? Just one of you to start with, but if you're successful, there'll be work for both of you.'

The elder brother thought for a moment and said, 'No, you give this job my sister. She speak English very good.'

The Englishman's eyes widened slightly. 'You want to give the job to your sister?'

Chen smiled. 'Yes. She very beautiful, very clever. You give her job. Very soon you rich. Very soon we all have job. Very soon we all rich. You need us. You understand – how you say? – bugger all about China peoples, China culture.'

The Japanese Girl

Reg had been a good teacher, but was surplus to needs at his current site, so the Department of Education had moved him to another school.

It was Justin's duty to oversee the school's information technology and he was responsible for the regular archiving of the school computer networks. Reg had been a very capable and industrious teacher of information technology, who had inspired his students with a lot of creative and useful material.

After some time, Justin thought it might be worth going through the archives to recover any useful ideas and resources in Reg's folders and files. To his consternation, he discovered in the back-up files a number of photos of one of Reg's students. It was impossible to comment on the girl's clothing as she was wearing none.

She was an attractive Japanese girl. Although it was not possible to tell her age from the photos, she was well into puberty. She appeared completely unstressed and quite happy to reveal her assets. In fact, her direct smile, straight into the eyes of the viewer, was something of an invitation to all comers. This was, of course, completely irrelevant, seeing that Reg should not have been in possession of any such photographs of his students.

This discovery created something of a problem for Justin. He should have reported the matter immediately to the school and the police. However, Justin quite liked Reg and hesitated to ruin his former colleague's life because of what may have been one unfortunate lapse in judgement. He spent some weeks going back to the photos and wondering about Reg and the girl. Justin convinced himself that he was just thinking about what he should do and that he was not in any way interested in the girl or stimulated by the photos. He did not, however, tell his colleagues or his wife, Helen, about the issue.

Justin obsessed over the matter for some six months. He was not dwelling so much on the legalities of it; in his dreams he was imagining the photo shoot. He wondered if it had been Reg himself who took the photos, and if Reg or the photographer had got lucky with the girl. In the end, Justin could not sleep at night, but was still daydreaming about the whole thing. In daydreams, he had more control over what was happening.

The file contained the student's name and the school still had her family address and phone number in Tokyo. Justin wallowed in his daydreams and fantasies for several weeks longer. Finally, fortified by regular viewings of the photographs, he made the phone call.

'*Moshi moshi. Mori desu.*' It was a Mr Mori, maybe her father.

Justin asked if there was a Suki at this number.

Realising the caller was an English-speaker, the man replied in halting English with a thick Japanese accent, 'You, please, wait now.'

Justin waited.

Then a voice at the other end sounded more American than Australian. 'Hello, who is this, please?'

'You may not remember me. My name is Reg,' he lied. 'I'm phoning you from Australia.'

'Reg? I don't know anyone called Reg. How do you know me?'

'Well, I'm sitting here looking at these photographs of you, and I know you better than most people because I'm seeing you without your clothes on.' Justin was sweating and his heart was racing.

'Without my clothes? What do you mean, without my clothes?'

'Well, these are photos of you without your clothes, and you're looking pretty good to me.'

There was a click followed by dial tone. Justin phoned back immediately.

The girl answered straight away. 'Hello, who are you?'

'It's Reg,' Justin continued. Reg was clearly the key to this girl's lock. 'I just thought I'd like to know you better. Do you have any more photos?'

'No more photos. What you want?'

'I thought maybe I'd like you. Are you coming back to Australia some time?'

'No, I will stay in Japan now.'

'How about if I come to Japan? Can we meet?'

Her voice dropped. 'No, you mustn't come. My parents will be very angry.' The other man may have come back into the room. 'I can't talk now,' she whispered huskily. 'You phone me here tomorrow afternoon.'

Justin did. He had expected the girl would be extremely nervous, but she had summoned up her nerve and presented herself calmly. Justin looked again at the photos and realised this was a very confident young girl, if not a woman.

'You will come to Japan?' she asked.

'I'll need some time to organise it, but I can.' The whole conversation was surreal, like something out of a movie. Justin had difficulty believing he was part of it.

However, he was committed. On the Internet, he found information about a January conference in Japan for Australian and Japanese teachers of English. January would be the long summer holiday in Australia. He enrolled through his workplace so that he could claim the trip on his income tax. His wife was interested in going with him, but he convinced her it would be boring. He could take some long service leave later in the year and they would go to Bali or Thailand. She still wanted to go to Japan, but said later in the year would be OK. He booked the January tickets to Japan and the hotel in Tokyo.

*

It was after midnight and there was a knock at Justin's hotel door. He went to the door. It was Suki. She didn't wait to be invited. She walked straight in.

'Who are you? You are not Reg.'

'No, I'm not Reg, but it doesn't matter.'

'You are right. It doesn't matter,' she said, producing a bottle. 'Do you know sake? We will make love, but first we will drink sake.'

And they did, but the lovemaking was not as heroic as Justin had hoped. Suki launched herself into the occasion with youthful enthusiasm and made a three-minute job of him.

'*Heiki desu. Shinpai shinaide.* It's OK, don't worry,' she said cheerfully and reached for the bedside bottle of sake. 'We will drink and we will make love again.'

And so they drank.

She drank less, saying, 'I, Japanese girl, cannot drink like you, Western man.'

However, she dutifully topped up Justin's glass several times. Somewhere in amongst it all, they made lust again, this time less embarrassingly for Justin. They drank again and Justin started to feel dizzy.

'Doesn't matter,' she said. 'Maybe you need fresh air. We will go out on the balcony. Then we will come back and make love again.'

*

Back in Australia, Reg was sitting at the breakfast table, reading the newspaper. His wife was still eating. The article was not prominent, page five, but it drew his attention.

'Hey, honey. Justin's dead. Seems he was drunk in a Tokyo hotel room and fell off the balcony.'

'Justin in Japan? Has he ever expressed an interest in Japan? What was he doing there?'

'No idea, love.'

Initiation

63

I have spent a lot of my life surrounded by men who needed to hit each other and I have usually not become involved. On my first day of high school, however, I found myself unable to avoid a very unpleasant person.

Those were the days of initiation, victimisation and bullying, although I'm not sure much has changed. I remember there was a tall, hefty lad who had singled me out and found some pretext to be unfriendly.

Observation in primary school and on the street had by then taught me that, if two people were of unequal size, the first blow was the best one. Consequently, the blow was upward.

I was not expecting the matter to be resolved with a single blow. However, the boy folded immediately and was rolling around on the ground, holding his face. My hand was stinging and I looked down and realised that the blood on my knuckles was my own. How did that happen?

'You bastard! Don't you know you should never hit anyone with bands?'

Bands? I thought. What are bands? I subsequently learnt that this was something rich kids got if they had ugly teeth and their parents could afford a clever dentist. No one in our neighbourhood had bands on his choppers.

The deputy principal knew that I had been the target of bullying, but also knew what the incident was going to cost the boy's parents. I was therefore given a jolly good caning to teach me that violence doesn't solve anything.

Where the Hell is Heaven?

It was going to be a big night in Elysia, one of the more elite localities on Mt Olympo in the galaxy of Blork. The local god, Pongo, had invited all the nicest deities in the universe to help him celebrate his birthday. Mortals sometimes struggle a little with the concept of gods having birthdays.

As his postman said to him a few days before the grand event, 'Birthday? What do you mean birthday? When do you have a birthday?'

'You'd be lucky to see one of them. According to the clock rate of some galaxies, they're millennia apart.'

'But how can you have a birthday? What do you mean "born"? How can you have been born?'

'My dear boy, same as you, same as everyone, same as everything. You can't have population without copulation.'

'But who was there to do the copulating? Weren't you the First Dude? Didn't you create everything?'

'Don't be silly, Boyo. People always seem to struggle with this in all the heavenly kingdoms. It's just like those Earthlings. Their goddites argued that my cousin must exist *a prima causa*. They said everything must have a cause, an origin, and the origin was god. Then some of them said, "What a load of bollocks. If everything must have a cause, then who invented god?"'

'So who's right then?'

'They all are, old chap. They get into such a flap about it, kill each other and everything. Of course there has to be a cause for everything. We gods did it. And we gods were created when our parents bonked each other.'

'Your parents?'

'Of course, my boy. Who else?'

'So where are they now?'

'Well, my mother's gone shopping. Not that she's in need of anything, and not that she needs any money to buy things. She's a goddess. People just give her stuff. She always gets what she wants.'

'And your father?'

'Yes, that's a bit of a story, actually. He's in hiding.'

'In hiding?'

'Yes, it's really been a bit boring for him, given Mother's obsession with shopping. He'd been hoping to give me a brother. Anyway, what with Mummy's eternal gadding about the universe, shopping, he slipped away to this Earth place and had it off with their god's wife, Ethel.'

'Earth's god has a wife?'

'Well, of course. How do you think all this creation takes place, old boy? Even we gods can't make something out of nothing. It's true that the Earthlings were a bit sexist about the whole thing. Absolute phallocracy in fact. For millennia, their women were in penile servitude, but you can't expect much more of their men. Most of them are complete thugs.'

'So is your father still there?'

'No, it seems that Ahmad discovered about his wife Ethel with my father, and he became fairly agitated. Daddy and Ethel shot through together to another galaxy. Ahmad was fairly pooey about the whole thing for some time and took it out on the Earthlings. Let some really ugly stuff happen. Now Ahmad's gone AWOL on them. He's off somewhere in search of Father and Ethel.'

'So are there any other gods left in this Earth place? Does Ahmad have parents?'

'Of course he does, but they're retired in some place called the Bahamas.'

'And what does your mother think about all this?'

'She knows nothing about it. She's still off shopping somewhere.'